T0142534

Love in a Far Country

Bernard C. Barton

Order this book online at www.trafford.com
or email orders@trafford.com

Most Trafford titles are also available at major online book retailers.

© Copyright 2009 Bernard Barton.
Edited by Shirley Shields.
Photography by Callen G. Barton.

Note for Librarians: A cataloguing record for this book is available from Library
and Archives Canada at www.collectionscanada.ca/amicus/index-e.html

Printed in Victoria, BC, Canada.

ISBN: 978-1-4251-8777-4 (Soft)

*We at Trafford believe that it is the responsibility of us all, as both individuals
and corporations, to make choices that are environmentally and socially sound.
You, in turn, are supporting this responsible conduct each time you purchase a
Trafford book, or make use of our publishing services. To find out how you are
helping, please visit www.trafford.com/responsiblepublishing.html*

*Our mission is to efficiently provide the world's finest, most comprehensive
book publishing service, enabling every author to experience success.
To find out how to publish your book, your way, and have it available
worldwide, visit us online at www.trafford.com*

Trafford rev. 10/21/2009

North America & international
toll-free: 1 888 232 4444 (USA & Canada)
phone: 250 383 6864 ♦ fax: 812 355 4082 ♦ email: info@trafford.com

JANET SINCLAIR WAS NO BEAUTY, though by her own admission, she could hardly be described as plain. She knew her nose was too long, and her lips were too thin, but her eyes were her redeeming feature. Almond-shaped, and dark, they were accentuated by long, dark lashes. In high heels, which gave her an enviable leggy appearance, she was significantly taller than most women, and not a few men had to look up to her. Her reticent nature resulted from her upbringing. Both parents were decidedly shy, and had nurtured few, if any, close friends, though Elsie Sinclair was by far the more outgoing of the two. There was about her firm, full figure a sensuousness that attracted men, and evoked envy in women. For a time she had a very secret affair, but her lover disappeared suddenly and unexpectedly. Then, very much on the rebound, she met William George Sinclair. He was a short, slight man, whose singular features were his dark, wavy hair, and dark eyes. Initially, they were what attracted Elsie, his wife, to him. Their courtship was hardly passionate, and after eighteen months, they married in a small, historic Protestant church close to their homes. Too quickly, they settled into a rather sedentary life. Elsie found occasional relief from her social inactivity by meeting for tea, coffee with a small group of women who commiserated with one another over their lack of connubial bliss. Sadly, Elsie Sinclair was finding her husband to be the stereotypical civil servant. Often he would dampen his wife's more effusive personality:

"My dear, I think a little less enthusiasm would be more appropriate," he commented on one occasion, and Elsie smiled at him indulgently.

When Elsie announced she was pregnant, one of the women

quipped, "Well Willie must have been having a few enjoyable moments in your marriage." There was an outburst of laughter, and Elsie blushed.

Over the years, Elsie Sinclair developed a close relationship with her daughter. By the time Janet entered college, the two of them had spent many hours in quite intimate conversation. Her father was interested in only what she intended to study and why, and what she intended to do after graduation. Once, he cautioned her about young men eager for a date.

"All too often they have one thing in mind," he said, although he never elaborated on the "thing."

Janet studied hard, graduated with first class honours, and never did date any young men with only "one thing in mind." She soon learned that a history degree was no introduction to lucrative employment, and she wanted the means to be truly independent. She did not want the subsidy provided by domestic residence, especially as her father was too controlling an influence. Too often he lectured her on the need to find a suitable mate of good reputation, and gainfully employed, who would bring stability to her life. He avoided the issue of marital bliss, because, Janet believed, this was not a vital aspect of her parents' marriage. Between them there was never any demonstrable display of affection. Janet vowed that whatever her personal defects, passion would not be lacking in her marriage.

A competent typist with a penchant for organization, Janet found employment with a prestigious London law firm. One of the partners recognized her strengths, and asked if she would like to be his personal secretary. Flattered by the request, Janet readily agreed, and quickly justified the partner's choice. Her competence earned her attractive bonuses, and she began to enjoy her newfound freedoms. She found a flat in the Chelsea area, and happily ended her daily train commute from Estley, as well as her domestic residency. Predictably, this move to full independence prompted her father to remark sarcastically, "I suppose now, you'll be entertaining a variety of male guests."

"Well father, you're always reminding me of the need to select a suitable mate."

"Yes, one of good reputation," he answered stiffly.

"And what makes you think my male guests will not have good reputations?"

"Well my dear, young people today seem to practice a looser morality."

"Well father, you'll just have to trust me."

"But you're so inexperienced."

"So, here's my opportunity to go into that big world and gain some experience," Janet replied impatiently.

"Yes, but don't be in too much of a hurry, my dear."

Just then, Janet's mother appeared. "I wish you two wouldn't argue so. I find it so upsetting."

"Well mother, I'll soon be out of here, and you'll be saved the arguments."

Her father looked at her sullenly, and left the room.

"I'll miss you. You know that, don't you?" said her mother tearfully.

"Yes mother, I do, but this move will be good for me." She hugged her mother, and added, "I have some packing to do."

"If you don't mind dear, I'll come and help you."

"Thanks. I'd appreciate that." This gave Elsie Sinclair an opportunity to be alone with her daughter.

"He means well, your father. He's just not good at expressing his feelings tactfully."

"That's for sure, mum. I still think this move is one of the best things I can do."

"You're probably right dear, but don't forget us."

"I wont, mum. In fact, you'll have to come up, and spend a weekend with me. We'll go out for dinner," said Janet enthusiastically.

"I'd like that, dear," her mother smiled

Edward Goodwin, a senior partner in the law firm Compton,

Goodwin, and James, had an enviable record for litigation. Some said he was driven, but others, more objective, merely pointed out he loved the practice of law, and was gifted. Janet Sinclair believed the latter, and derived a particular pleasure from working for him. She was paid well for meeting Edward Goodwin's exacting standard. She enjoyed the challenge, and Edward Goodwin was quick to compliment Janet on her work. The jealousy of others toward one so new to the secretarial pool, merely motivated Janet to further excel.

"Miss Sinclair learns amazingly fast," Edward Goodwin confided to a colleague one afternoon. At the time, she had been working for him only three weeks, and he was commenting upon not only the speed and accuracy of her work, but also her grasp of the law he practiced.

"I really think she should consider law as a career." Edward was talking with his partner, Keith Compton.

"You pay her well, Edward, so maybe she enjoys the money without the additional demands of the practice of law."

"Yes, that could be true, Keith, but she's a bright young lady, and I like to think she has ambition beyond being my personal secretary."

Janet was not a little flattered, when a few weeks later, Edward Goodwin asked her if she had ever considered studying law.

"Actually, Mr. Goodwin, I haven't. I've been enjoying my work with you, and all I've been able to do because of the generous salary you pay me."

"You mean I should reduce it, and then you might consider law?" Mr. Goodwin laughed as Janet's face showed surprise

"Oh, Mr. Goodwin, you wouldn't do that?" and Janet smiled coyly.

"With your speed and quality of work? Never. But do think about my suggestion. The firm can certainly help you."

"Thank you, Mr. Goodwin. I will consider your suggestion."

One thing Janet had learned from her father was frugality. However, for her this meant saving a portion of her salary, and establishing a fund that would grow with added interest. Within a month of Janet's settling into her apartment, her mother visited her. She arrived early one Friday evening, and the two of them dined on food Janet bought at a nearby delicatessen. Elsie particularly appreciated the wine.

"Wine goes so well with a dinner," said Elsie, a faint smile on her lips.

"You never have any?"

"No, your father considers it an extravagance."

"Oh, that's nonsense," replied Janet, notably irritated. "You and dad need to bring some enjoyment into your lives."

"You're so right dear. We don't go anywhere. Your father has no interest in the theatre or concerts."

"That reminds me," interrupted Janet excitedly, "I have tickets for tomorrow's concert at the Festival Theatre. I thought we could have dinner there, then take in the concert."

"Oh, my dear, that sounds wonderful. I feel I'm beginning to live." Elsie's face brightened, and she squeezed Janet's hands affectionately.

"The concert's all Mozart. You'll love it, mum."

Elsie enjoyed both the dinner and the concert. Sipping a cream sherry after the concert, she remarked, "I can't remember the last time I did anything like this. Thank you so much Janet. It's been a wonderful evening."

"Mum," replied Janet earnestly, "you need to do something like this more often."

"You're right, dear, but with whom? Certainly not with your father, he's just not interested. A visit to the local, that's about it for him."

"Mum, do you ever think you made the wrong choice with Dad?"

Smiling wistfully, Elsie Sinclair looked at her daughter. "Oh, sometimes I do. I see our drifting further apart. We just don't

5

do anything together. Your father seems to live in his own small world, and I'm never part of it."

"Doesn't he get any enjoyment out of life?"

"Oh, he still enjoys sex, but I know I don't give him what he wants." There was sadness in Elsie's voice.

"Men," snapped Janet. "Always ready, aren't they?"

"You've found that out in your young life, dear," replied her mother with a smile. "Shortly after you were born, your father had a vasectomy, and there was no stopping him."

"Obviously he wanted the sex without the children," said Janet, facetiously.

"You've got that right, dear. What are your memories of your father?"

"Nothing special. We never had a real conversation. He kept so much to himself. We never did anything together. He never taught me anything, like how to ride a bike, or play tennis, or swim. My friends' fathers did, but not mine," said Janet emphatically.

"Of course not, dear. He doesn't swim, and he's never played tennis, and come to think of it, I've never seen him ride a bike."

"By the time I was sixteen, and obviously a young woman, I often felt uncomfortable when he looked at me."

"That doesn't surprise me, Janet."

"You think he wanted to go to bed with me?" Janet asked surprised.

"Oh, I'm sure he thought about it," replied her mother almost matter- of- factly.

"You know, mum, I think you should divorce him. You'd be much happier."

"Yes, but what would I do? He has the money. The house is in joint ownership, and I suppose I could take my share. But how long would that last?"

"There must be something you can do," replied Janet, a little forlornly.

Over the ensuing months, Elsie Sinclair visited her daughter frequently. Her visits were the welcome break in the monotony of her otherwise humdrum life. William made snide remarks about her having male friends in London, which accounted for her numerous visits. Elsie challenged his accusation with a perfectly logical suggestion.

"Why don't you visit your daughter? Then the three of us could dine out, and go to a concert or a play."

William responded with predictable scorn.

"Is that how she's wasting her money?"

"Well, at least she's living," answered Elsie sarcastically.

"Oh, does that mean we aren't?"

"When did we last go out together? When did we last do anything together?" Elsie's voice trembled, and she began to cry.

William's mute response was a shrug of his thin shoulders as a gesture of indifference, and he left the room.

Janet surprised everyone at work, as well as her parents, when she announced she was going to Canada.

"Why do you want to go there?" she was asked. "What will you do?"

Her mother, especially, was saddened by the thought of Janet's leaving. Now there would be no weekends with her daughter to relieve the tedium of life with William. She began to contemplate divorce as an acceptable option.

Janet had a strong desire to travel, and she liked what she had read about British Columbia. Furthermore, the people there spoke English, and Canada was an easy country for a British subject to enter. As for work, she was confident about quickly finding a job. A young woman on the staff of British Columbia House wondered why she wanted to leave London for the west coast of Canada.

"I suppose I could ask why you left Canada to come here," replied Janet.

"You've never experienced an Alberta winter," was the prompt reply. "Furthermore, Edmonton isn't exactly London."

"Well, I'd like to see the Rockies, and something more than London's sprawl."

"Oh well, best of luck." The young woman smiled at Janet.

Her father debunked her immigrating to Canada. "What will you do there that you can't do here?" he asked angrily. "You'll probably run off with some lumberjack."

Elsie just smiled. She envied her daughter. In fact, she had considered joining Janet, but then realized she would be a handicap.

Shortly after nine o'clock in the morning of a late April day in 1954, the P and O steamship Acadia pulled slowly away from the Southampton dock, and began its voyage to Quebec City, almost four thousand miles across the Atlantic. Janet stood against the rail, and watched the few people on the dock grow smaller and smaller. She waved at no one in particular. A young woman beside her quietly uttered her doubts about departing,

"Oh God. What the hell am I doing on this ship?" She laughed softly, looked at Janet, and flicked a half-burned cigarette into the water.

"Well," replied Janet, "I know what I'm doing, and right now I'm going to get some breakfast." With that, she left her confused fellow passenger, and made her way to the dining room.

Very early on the voyage, Janet received the close attention of a number of young Canadian hockey players, N.H.L. rejects mostly, though some had played in the American Hockey League. They now played for teams in the English Hockey League, and for teams in European countries, which welcomed these aggressive Canadian players, many of whom still dreamed of making it to the National Hockey League. They were hard living young men, and Janet had to fend off some with decidedly ulterior motives. They voiced their frustration with such epithets as "frigid bitch," and "the ice bitch," but Janet was not going to become the pregnant victim of a one-night affair in the middle of the Atlantic.

Nevertheless, the crossing had its pleasant moments. She met other young women destined for British Columbia. One of them, Claire Dempsey, a vivacious, attractive woman, had survived similar assaults on her virginity, and readily confided in Janet.

"My God, Janet, I hope it's not going to be like this all the way to Vancouver," said Claire, with a wide grin.

"I think the train will be something of a sanctuary," relied Janet.

Claire was distancing herself from a romance that had failed, largely because of sexual differences.

"Men seem to have one thing on their minds," said Claire.

"Sex," interjected Janet, and they both laughed.

"Do you think there are men out there with something other than sex on their minds?" asked Claire.

"I like to think so," replied Janet. "I like to think there are men who have other than ulterior motives."

"So, Janet," exclaimed Claire, arms spread wide, "let's go look for them in our new country. We just may be lucky, " and she threw her arms around a rather startled Janet.

Claire was joining a friend in Kitimat. "She's been there six months, and is saving thousands of dollars. I'll be working in the same office." Then, with an enthusiasm that was infectious, exclaimed, "Janet, why don't you join me? We'll fly to Kitimat together. I'm sure there's a job there for you. In fact, I have the Company's Vancouver address. Why don't we go there when we arrive in Vancouver?"

Unaccustomed to such enthusiasm, Janet looked a little overwhelmed. Claire was holding both her hands, and Janet was looking into a pair of sparkling blue eyes.

"Claire, you're on," said Janet, a broad smile on her lips.

By now the train was making its torturous way through the mountains of British Columbia. The two of them marveled at the engineering feats of the spiral tunnels, and gazed, fascinated at the jagged sandstone hills, carved by decades of melting snow, that paralleled the railroad east of Kamloops. But Janet felt a strange yearning for the prairies. There was something restful about the vast swell of that land. Never had she seen such endless horizons, or experienced the lingering crimson of a prairie sunset. For her, there was a peacefulness about this immense landscape. This British Columbia presented a restless contrast. Dawn found them traveling above the Fraser River in its changing moods, as it churned through the canyon, then made the big ninety degree turn at Hope, entered the wide, green valley, and continued quietly on to the ocean. Janet and Claire were full of nervous anticipation. After almost eight days, their long journey across an ocean and a continent was finally ending. Janet looked at Claire, a nervous smile on her lips, and asked,

"Claire, you think the Company will have a job for me?"

"I'm sure you'll have no difficulty getting one. Personal secretary to a senior partner in a London law firm. Darling, they'll probably assign you to the president of the Company."

They looked at each other, and burst out laughing. It was a release of nervous energy.

"But Claire, they might think I'm unsuited to life in a pioneer aluminium town. Dirt roads, no theatres, or upscale restaurants."

"Just tell them it's character building. And by the way, Janet, get use to saying 'aluminum.' Drop the final 'i.'" Claire grinned at Janet.

"Maybe you should accompany me, when I apply."

"Ah Janet, they'll charter a flight for you."

"I think they'll put me on a slow boat to this aluminum town." Janet had a broad grin on her face as she gave exaggerated emphasis to aluminum.

"You're learning, kido."

At nine o'clock the big diesel slid quietly into the elegant C.P.R. terminal at the foot of Granville Street.

Asking for directions to the Aluminum Company offices,

Claire and Janet were pleased to learn they had to walk only three blocks. Before going, they decided to have a coffee.

They sat at the counter of a small café, and quickly engaged the young waitress in conversation.

"So you're going to Kitimat," she said. "You know, that's where I should go, and make some money, instead of earning nickels and dimes here."

"Can you do office work?" asked Claire.

"No. Left school when I was sixteen, and all I've done is waitress in small joints like this. I have to change some to work in a classy restaurant."

Claire looked at her sympathetically. "Maybe you could find something in Kitimat that would pay more, and you could learn some new skills, like typing. Oh God, I'm giving career counseling, and I've just arrived here."

Next moment, the three of them were laughing.

"You know," said the waitress, "I need someone like you. Someone to get me out of my rut, and motivate me."

"What's your name?" asked Claire.

"Corinne. Corinne Kozacks."

"I'm Claire Dempsey, and this is my friend, Janet Sinclair. We met on the boat coming over, and I've persuaded Janet to join me in Kitimat. We arrived in Vancouver this morning, bright, eager immigrants."

"You know, I've never left Vancouver. Well, I've been to New Westminster, but I haven't done like you. Really traveled. Left the country. I've yet to go to Vancouver Island."

"Is that far?" asked Claire.

"Oh, a couple of hours on the ferry," replied Corinne.

"Corinne, why don't you quit this job, and come to Kitimat with us?" asked Claire. "We're going to the Company offices, and I could enquire for you. First class short-order cook looking for work in Kitimat," Claire uttered enthusiastically.

"I don't think I could leave so soon," said Corinne, looking a little disconsolate. "I'd need a replacement."

"I'm sure there's someone to fill your place," Claire added.

"First class," replied Corinne, smiling.

"Oh, touché." Claire chuckled. 'Well, your replacement need not be quite as good as you. Just experienced."

Janet observed this whole incident, intrigued. "Claire, what if Corinne is the sole support for her mother?"

"No Janet. My mother died six months ago, and I've no idea where my father is. He left the family six years ago."

"I'm sorry to hear that. Men!" uttered Janet. "You just can't trust them," she added in a low, sharp voice.

"Well, Corinne," said Claire, "I think this move would be good for you. What do you say? We'll enquire, and come back, and let you know."

"This is all so sudden, but if there's a job, I think I can join you ladies," said Corinne, clearly overwhelmed by this unexpected event in her quiet life.

Cameron Jarvis was the young, energetic personnel manager for Alcan's Vancouver office. An M.A. in industrial psychology, he was forward thinking, and greatly respected by senior management. When Janet and Claire entered his office, he greeted them warmly,

"Good morning ladies. I understand you arrived in Vancouver only this morning?"

"That's correct," replied Claire.

"You must be tired after nearly three days on the train."

"You know," began Claire, "I think we're too excited to be tired. That will come later."

Cameron Jarvis shook his head, and smiled. "I'm impressed. You've come all this way. No family, no friends here. You have an adventurous spirit."

"Well. I do have a job in Kitimat. In fact I'm joining a friend there, and being an optimist, I've convinced Janet there's a job for her too, in Kitimat." Then smiling coyly at Cameron Jarvis, she added, "And you're going to tell me I'm right."

Cameron Jarvis's usual objective, professional demeanour wilted before Claire's charm, and sparkling blue eyes.

"Now, which one of you is Miss Dempsey?"

"I am." Claire smiled.

"And you must be Miss Sinclair?"

Janet smiled in acknowledgement. Looking at her, Cameron Jarvis began to regain his composure.

"Do you have any references, Miss Sinclair?"

"Yes, I do, Mr. Jarvis," and reaching into her large purse, she withdrew a long manila envelope, and handed it to him.

"Miss. Sinclair, while I read this letter, I'll have you fill out an application form." He reached into a side draw of his capacious desk, and handed Janet a long form. Then he rose, and directed her to a side room. "You'll find pens, pencils, and erasers on the table. Make yourself comfortable, and take your time."

Janet was surprised at the opulence of the room. The floor was thickly carpeted. Against the wall facing the door was a teak bookcase. In the center was a low teak coffee table, and to the right was a round teak table, with two padded chairs. On the walls were prints of Renoir and Degas, all to make hopeful applicants feel welcome. Janet took her time, and when she returned the form to Cameron Jarvis, he had finished reading Edward Goodwin's lengthy letter.

"Very impressive credentials, Miss. Sinclair, and a strong recommendation from a senior partner."

"Thank you." Janet smiled politely.

"While you will not find the same challenge in Kitimat, there most certainly is a job, if you so wish," said Cameron Jarvis, as he handed Janet her reference.

"Very much so, Mr. Jarvis. I think I will enjoy the experience."

"Well, it will be very different from London. Now ladies, there is a plane leaving Coal Harbour for Kitimat at nine o'clock Friday morning. Where are you staying?"

"At the Y.W.C.A.," replied Janet.

"O.K. I'm going to give you money for a taxi to Coal Harbour. It's a short ride."

Then Claire interrupted quietly. "Mr. Jarvis, we have a request to make."

He looked at Claire, and smiled. "Go ahead."

"Would you know if there are any openings in Kitimat for a short-order cook? We met this young woman who desperately wants to get away from the city. When we told her where we were going, she asked if we would enquire for her."

Janet wanted to smile at Claire's exaggeration of the truth.

"I don't do the hiring for kitchen staff, but I believe there presently are openings in one of the kitchens. I'll make enquiries, and phone you at the Y early this afternoon." Cameron Jarvis had a smile on his face as he rose. "Ladies, it's been a pleasure. I hope things go well for you in Kitimat. It's beautiful country. I'll be in touch later today, hopefully with good news." He shook hands warmly, and saw them out to the spacious hallway. In the elevator going down, Claire was exuberant.

"Janet, first day in Vancouver and you've got a job, and I'm betting Corinne will have one before the day's out."

Janet looked at Claire. "And guess what Claire?"

"What," said Claire, her eyes wide open.

"Mr. Jarvis has a crush on you. I think you're going to see more of him."

"You do," replied Claire, a little surprised. "I must admit, he was rather sweet, and quite handsome. Do you think he might be an exception?"

"An exception?" queried Janet.

"Yes. You know. He might have something other than sex on his mind."

Janet burst out laughing, and Claire joined in. They stepped out of the elevator, and into the pale sunlight of a May morning.

At three-thirty that afternoon, the anticipated phone call came. The news was good. There was an opening for an experienced short-order cook, and Cameron Jarvis gave Claire the name of a contact in Kitimat. It seemed Corinne would be a cook in training simply because of the size of the operation. Having thanked Cameron, Claire quickly phoned Corinne at the café, and told her the good news. Corinne was excited. Already, she had informed her boss she was considering going to Kitimat, and, surprisingly, he encouraged her.

"Corinne, I think that's a good move. You've been working here long enough. It's time for you to get out, and go elsewhere, and Kitimat's a good choice. You'll make more money than I can pay you. Good luck. Send me a card occasionally." He hugged her, and bade her a tearful goodbye. "I'll miss you. You've been a good worker." She left without looking back.

Later that evening, Corinne phoned Claire, and told her she had quit her job with the owner's blessing. "He actually encouraged me. Felt it was time for me to get out and go somewhere else. I want to thank you for giving me a push. I needed that."

"Corinne, I'm so pleased for you. Now be at the Y at eight o'clock Friday morning. We fly out at nine o'clock from Coal Harbour."

"I'll be there, if I have to crawl."

"You don't have to be that desperate, Corinne. Just take a taxi." Claire laughed.

"See you Friday morning. Good night, Claire."

"Good night, Corinne." Claire turned to Janet. "So, it's all set. The three of us fly to Kitimat on Friday. A whole new stage of our lives is about to begin," said Claire, excitedly.

Janet was strangely quiet as she looked at Claire, and said, "Don't you wonder what's in store for us?"

"Oh, Janet, dear, I think it's all very exciting."

They slept well that night. The day had been long and eventful.

Shortly after nine, the float- plane lifted off the placid water of Coal Harbour, and climbed into a cloudless sky. The three young women were treated to the majestic beauty of the snow-mantled Coast Mountains that line the deep inlets along the coast, and disappear into the dark interior. Then it seemed all too soon the plane was sliding smoothly over the water lapping the shores of Kitimat. An Alcan employee awaited Claire, Janet, and Corinne, and quickly drove them to their residence, showed Claire, and Janet the building where they would be working, and gave Corinne directions where to meet her contact person.

"Just think," said Corinne, "three days ago I was behind a counter wondering if I would ever find the initiative to do anything else. Now I'm in Kitimat about to begin something new, and all thanks to you Claire."

"I'm so glad you're here," replied Claire.

"Well ladies," interjected Janet, "lets check into the Ritz Carlton."

"But my dear, think of all the money we're going to save," chuckled Claire.

One week after the three young women arrived in Kitimat, Cameron Jarvis found cause for a business appointment in that same town. The float- plane touched down on the calm waters of the long Douglas Channel in brilliant sunshine. Coincidentally, his appointment was in the same building where Claire and Janet were settling into the office routine with notable efficiency. The discerning reader will not be surprised to learn that Cameron Jarvis was fully aware of their presence, and it will come as no surprise that he visited them shortly after concluding his business. That he also invited Claire to dine with him that evening is what the same perceptive reader would have anticipated. In the less than elegant environs of the Kitimat Hotel, there began a romance that resulted some thirteen months later in Claire Dempsey's assuming the name Claire Jarvis. Doubtless, this relationship could be considered a whirlwind romance, for Cameron Jarvis fell under the entrancing spell of Claire's magnetic personality, just as much as she was captivated by his charming ingenuousness, and gracious courtesy. Janet was highly supportive of this romance, and had she not been diverted by an equally consuming one, she would have been Claire's maid-of-honour at her wedding the following June. It seems Kitimat was their Camelot, where each found her Sir Gawain. In the months leading up to June, Claire was a welcome guest, at least once a month, at the Jarvis household. Mrs. Jarvis was especially delighted at the prospect of Claire becoming her daughter-in-law.

Janet's Sir Gawain was another colonial, but this one was a long way from home. Ron McCabe was a stocky Australian, with a sardonic smile. He was in the final months of a two-year stay in Kitimat, and was pleased to say his bank account had grown appreciably during that time. He planned to return home in the late summer, and help his brother with the winery on the south side of the Murray River. Thirty-five thousand dollars would provide a significant boost to the operation of the winery. Two years in the confines of Kitimat could do strange things to the psyche. For over eighteen months Ron had adapted to a routine of long working days. He accepted all the overtime offered him, and only occasionally took a day off. He read voraciously, and wrote weekly to his family, but he missed the company of women. They were in Kitimat, but most were simply passing through. Kitimat provided a hiatus that enabled them to accumulate the finances for their next destination, usually more exotic than this aluminum town on the central coast of British Columbia. Janet Sinclair was different. She was in no particular hurry. In fact, she wasn't even sure of her next destination. She met Ron at a beach party one Sunday afternoon in late June. The exceptional warmth of this early summer day was conducive to conversation, and Ron and Janet talked for a long time. He grew up in an atmosphere of marital harmony, which resulted in four well- adjusted adult children. "My parents laughed a lot together," he told Janet.

"How wonderful," she replied. "Mine hardly spoke to each other."

"I'm sorry to hear that. It's so important to grow up in a family where there's love and laughter."

"Well Ron, you were most fortunate."

"You've done well in spite of having parents who hardly spoke to each other." Ron smiled at Janet.

"My mother was the difference. We have a close relationship. While I was in London, we had some wonderful weekends together. Theatre, concerts, dinners out." There was a note of nostalgia in her voice.

"Thank God for mothers," said Ron. "They bring us into this world, and never stop loving us. Well Janet, it's time for a little tucker." He grinned at Janet, who looked puzzled." That's Oz for food."

Over the next month, they saw a lot of each other. Janet realized she was growing to like this congenial Australian. A rather hasty engagement while in London had an equally hasty conclusion, when her fiancé decided she lacked both the extroversion and social background essential in his potential spouse.

"Oh, those stuffy Limeys, still fussing over family background, and the school you went to. No offence, Janet," Ron laughed.

"None taken. I was pleased to leave all that."

Accessibility only by air or water merely accentuated Kitimat's isolation. The hot, dry summer of '54 drifted by lazily. Dust rose thick from Kitimat's dirt roads, and coated the trees and shrubs bordering them. For Claire and Janet this was a summer to remember. They lived in that euphoric state of romantic love, each convinced she had found her man, her lifetime partner. Theirs was a blissful state, envied by some, but viewed with skepticism by others. Ron was more constrained. He viewed love as something personal and private, and he delighted more in those times when he and Janet were together. He expressed his love in an indirect way, in his ambitious plans for the winery, and how Janet could be a significant part of those plans.

"Oh Janet, I have such ambitious plans for the winery. I

envision its being, if not the biggest in Victoria, at least the best. I get excited thinking about it." A smile lit up his face as he looked at Janet.

"The winery means a lot to you, doesn't it Ron?"

"It's everything. Well, almost everything," and he looked self-consciously at Janet.

"Are you telling me I'm part of that 'everything'?"

"I guess I am," and Ron squeezed Janet's hands gently.

Looking into Ron's eyes, Janet said, "I love you Ron, and I want to be a part of your life."

Without saying a word, Ron let go of Janet's hands, and slowly embraced her. She remained silent, relishing the intimacy of the moment.

Living on the east side of the Kitimaat River, Corinne saw little of Janet and Claire, who lived and worked three miles away, on the west side of the river. However, in late July, when Corinne was promoted to Assistant Manager of Cafeteria Operations, she knew she had to share her good news with her two friends. On a warm evening, late in July, Corinne knocked on the door of Claire's room. There was an immediate stirring inside. The door opened wide, and a surprised and smiling Claire greeted Corinne exuberantly.

"Corinne, how good to see you. I'm sure we have lots to talk about."

"Oh, I think we do," replied Corinne, growing visibly excited. "I've something exciting to tell you."

"Don't tell me! You're getting married."

"No. Better. But first, let's call on Janet, and I'll tell both of you over coffee." Corinne was becoming more excited.

"OK Corinne, let's go and rouse the sleeping beauty. She's probably flaked out on her bed. Then we'll go for coffee and dessert, and you can tell us your exciting news."

"I'd love to. I haven't seen Janet for so long."

They went quickly down to the ground floor. Claire rapped sharply on the door.

"Who is it?" asked a sleepy voice.

"Janet dear, it's me, Claire, with a visitor."

"Come in," came the sleepy reply.

The two entered. Stretched out on her bed, Janet slowly opened her eyes. Then she sat up suddenly.

"Why Corinne, what a pleasant surprise. We've neglected you, haven't we?"

"Oh, I'm just as much to blame. I've been busy."

"Janet dear," Claire interrupted impatiently, "Corinne has some wonderful news for us, but she insists on telling us over coffee."

"And before you say it Janet, I'm not getting married."

"Oh," uttered Janet with a smile. "Then you're pregnant," she added in a deadpan voice.

"Janet, I don't have a boy friend, and you know I'm not the promiscuous kind," Corinne scolded.

"But come on my dear. We're going for coffee and dessert." Claire was growing impatient

"OK, but let me first brush my hair, and put on my face."

"Janet, my dear, you look beautiful as you are. The men will still ogle you."

"I know," replied Janet with a conceited toss of her head, "but I'll only be a minute."

"By the way, this is my treat," said Corinne

The coffee shop was quiet when they entered. Each placed her order, and Corinne paid. Then they sat at a window table. Janet and Claire looked intently at Corinne.

"Now Corinne, tell us about your good news," demanded Claire.

"Well, I've been promoted. I'm now the Assistant Manager of Cafeteria Operations," answered Corinne excitedly. For a moment she sat looking at Claire and Janet, a broad smile on her face. Claire broke the short silence.

20

"Oh Corinne that's wonderful. Congratulations! You deserve it. You've worked so hard."

"Wow! That's quite a title," laughed Janet. "From cook to assistant manager in two and a half months. Pretty good, I'd say."

"Aren't you glad you took our advice, and came with us to Kitimat," said Claire proudly.

"Can't thank you enough. Best thing I've ever done."

"You're finally revealing your hidden talents."

"Take note, Corinne. This is your counselor speaking," teased Janet.

"But Janet, my dear, you have to admit, Corinne is better off than she was in that 'hole in the wall' in Vancouver."

"Touche Claire. But Corinne, tell us more about your promotion."

"Well, there's not a lot to say. I'll assist Kate with the day-to-day operation of the cafeteria. I'll note if a certain item on a menu proves unpopular, and find out why. You know, Janet, the job's about quality control, both food and service."

"Well, my dear," said Claire, "with you on the job, both will be excellent."

"Oh Claire, you have such confidence in me," Corinne sighed.

"I have every reason to. You need to be made aware of your talents."

"This is your counselor speaking," Janet repeated.

"And have I not given Corinne excellent advice?" replied Claire triumphantly.

"Claire, my dear, I truly believe you have missed your real calling," said Janet with an assumed seriousness.

"Janet, there are times when I could smack you," replied Claire, trying to appear angry. Then they looked at each other and laughed.

"OK, you two. Enough about my job, and Janet, stop harassing my favourite counselor, I want to hear about your love lives."

"Thank you for your support, Corinne," said Claire quietly. Janet just smiled.

"Well, Cameron is fine. He's er, well, a lovely man."

"Claire, you can do better than that. Surely this is a romantic time in your life?"

"Corinne," Janet interjected, "they're madly in love, and anytime soon I'm expecting Claire to announce a wedding date. Am I right Claire?"

"Oh Janet, dear, of course you are. This romance has all been so sudden, and yes, Cameron is a darling man, and I do love him. And too often I'm in an emotional spin." Claire became very emotional and teary-eyed. Corinne came and sat beside her, and put an arm around her.

"Oh Claire, I think this is wonderful. You're so fortunate to have met someone like Cameron."

"Thank you Corinne. I think so too. You know, it really is a wonderful feeling, and for all Janet's composure, she's experiencing the same condition. Right, my dear?" Claire, her face now wreathed in smiles, looked at Janet, who simply grinned, and nodded her head.

"Well, tell me more, Janet?"

"Well, Claire's perfectly correct. We're both emotional wrecks at times. Ron's a good man, but he's Australian, and Australian males aren't exactly attuned to the subtleties of romance. Romance is far more important to women than it is to men, Women enjoy holding hands and talking. Most men are too quick to embrace and jump into bed, and if the woman doesn't follow, they become irritated, and move on to the next available, willing female."

"You think all men are like that, Janet?"

"Oh, not all, of course not, but few approach romance the way most women do. Ron's a good man He's not trying to get me into bed. Fact is he's a strong Catholic, and does not believe in premarital sex."

"He's quite an exception," said Corinne in a surprised tone. "Is that true of Cameron?" She looked at Claire.

"As a matter of fact, it is, Corinne." We've really latched onto a couple of exceptions, haven't we Janet?"

"We have. But I'm not complaining, Sometimes chastity can save one from all sorts of problems and disappointments."

"Wise counseling my dear," Claire commented with a smile.

"So Janet, do you think you'll marry Ron?"

"If he asks me, yes."

"Which means you'll go to Australia with him?"

"Yes, it does, and I'll learn all about vineyards and wine making. I find the prospect quite exciting."

"But Australia is so far away," said Corinne softly. "Won't your parents miss you?"

"My mother, yes, but not my father. We never got on together. I'm certain he was glad when I left home and lived in London. I really think my mother would join me in Australia. She'd divorce my father, but he won't give her one."

"Why not?" Corinne asked.

"Because he's stubborn and miserable."

"Some men really are spiteful, aren't they?" added Claire.

"Ain't that the truth," said Corinne, with a faraway look. "I'll miss you if you go away, Janet."

"I'll miss you and Claire. Some good decisions have sad consequences, don't they?"

"Yes," said Corinne. "Claire, please don't go any farther away than Vancouver. Who else would I have to counsel me?" she chuckled.

"Now Corinne," began Claire, "don't tell us you've been living like a nun all these weeks."

"No. I've had coffee a few times in the cafeteria with a young electrician. Works for Alcan. An interesting man; loves to draw and paint."

"Have you seen any of his works?" asked Claire.

"Not yet. He's promised to show me some."

"But not in his room," interjected Janet, with a smile.

"No," replied Corinne, returning the smile. "He'll bring a sketch book, probably next Saturday."

"That's smart," said Janet. "No entering the lion's den."

"Oh Janet, I don't think he's that kind. He's of Polish descent. His last name is Madrewski. Has a brother a priest, and his sister is a nurse."

"Oh, serving the people," said Claire."

"Very altruistic," added Janet, somewhat flippantly.

"I'm glad you approve," said Corinne, rather facetiously.

"Oh Corinne, I hope you'll soon be experiencing what Janet and I are." Claire simply grinned at Corinne,

"Well, I'm not experiencing it yet," laughed Corinne.

"Just wait, my dear. You will," replied Claire with a dreamy look.

They talked a while longer, enjoying the pleasure of one another's company, and the intimate discourse peculiar to women, but Corinne left, saddened by the thought she was soon to lose a very dear friend.

That summer of love, of exalted, romantic moments continued through the warm, dry days of August. When Claire was not spending a weekend with Cameron at his family's home, she would join Janet and Ron for a beach party. In her absence, Janet and Ron enjoyed leisurely walks along the maze of trails surrounding Kitimat. They discovered quiet locations where they would sit and talk. Janet asked Ron a litany of questions about his family, ever conscious of their contrasting familial backgrounds, and envying him what he had experienced growing up.

"You're so fortunate to have grown up in such a family," she told Ron during one of their walks.

"You know, I guess I am, and I've never really thought much about it. Just took it for granted, though I've always appreciated my family."

"Claire has become the sister I never had," said Janet, gazing into the distance.

"Now don't tell me I'm the brother you never had," grinned Ron.

"Ron, how could you say that, after all I've told you?" and she pushed him playfully on his shoulder.

"Janet, you're very special to me." There was sincerity in Ron's voice.

"Thank you Ron," replied Janet, and jumping up, she shouted, "Come on! Let's walk down to the river, and then we'll have dinner at the Hotel."

In late August, Ron informed Janet that he would be leaving for Australia in two weeks' time.

"What I want to ask you, Janet is, would you like to come with me, and meet my family, and look around the winery?"

Scarcely concealing her excitement, Janet replied, "Oh, Ron, when do we leave? I mean, I'd love to meet your family. I think it will be a little overwhelming at first, but thank you for the invitation," and she threw her arms around him, and began to cry.

"Good. Then I'll buy two tickets to Sydney."

"Oh no, Ron. You don't have to buy my ticket. I have money."

"No. I'm inviting, and I'm paying. After two years in this isolation, I have a big bank account."

Janet looked at him, tears running down her cheeks, and a smile on her face. "Okay. You win." Her arms slid from his shoulders, and down to her sides. "I'm just so excited."

"Good," answered Ron. "I'll send the family a telegram to let them know we're coming. Meanwhile, start thinking about what you want to take with you, and what you can give away."

"Not much of either, Ron."

Two days later Claire had the offer of a job in Alcan's Vancouver office. Doubtless, Cameron Jarvis, operating discreetly in the background, had much to do with the offer. Claire was predictably quick to accept. One day after accepting the job, Claire informed Janet. "Oh, Janet, you'll never guess what's happened?"

"Don't tell me. You're pregnant."

"What! Of course not, that will only happen when I'm married. I have a job in the Vancouver office."

"It helps when you know the right people, doesn't it?" said Janet, flatly.

"Janet, my dear, you sound a little sour"

"No. I'm simply stating a truth."

"I'd love to have you join me, and I'll ask Cameron. You've become a dear friend," said Claire, taking hold of Janet's hands.

"Thank you Claire. I truly appreciate your friendship, and I'm glad for you, but actually, I have to decline your offer. Now I have something to tell you." Claire gazed at Janet's stomach. "No, Claire, I'm not pregnant. Ron's a very traditional Catholic. Sex only in marriage."

"Not like those hot-blooded Canadian hockey players," laughed Claire.

"No," smiled Janet. "But I have accepted his invitation to go with him to Australia, and meet his family."

"You have! Oh Janet, I'll miss you, Australia's so far away. When will I ever see you?" She was holding Janet's hands, and looking at her, teary-eyed.

"Claire, I may not stay there. Maybe I'll return to Canada."

"Janet dear, do you love Ron?"

Janet blushed. "Yes, I do. Something tells me I won't be returning."

"And something tells me you're right."

They stood for a moment, holding hands and crying. Then they were hugging each other, knowing it would be a long time before they would see each other again, indeed, wondering if they ever would.

While Claire was happy for Janet, she was saddened by the thought of her going so far away. Since meeting on board ship, and during their months together in Kitimat, Claire and Janet had formed a close friendship, something significantly lacking in Janet's young life. Janet appreciated Claire's joyful spontaneity, and her readiness to listen to Janet's concerns and expectations. Claire had become the sister Janet never had, and now their ways were to part.

The responses by Janet's parents to her going to Australia to meet Ron's parents, and stay at their home were predictable. Her mother was delighted she had met so "nice a young man," but her father grumbled about her "running off to Australia with a strange man. Young people today," he concluded, "have no morals." His subsequent adultery revealed his true hypocrisy. Elsie smiled, and said nothing.

Before leaving Kitimat, Janet met with Corinne to say goodbye. In the months Corinne had been in Kitimat, Janet had observed a remarkable blossoming in Corinne. She had become more assured of herself, and had acquired a confidence the young woman Janet first met in Vancouver did not have,

"You've grown, Corinne. You're a different person from the one who flew to Kitimat with Claire and me."

"You think so, Janet?"

"I know so. You'll do well here."

"Interesting you should say that. Doug wants me to be a partner in a café that's going to open next month in the Townsite. I would be the cook and assistant manager; he'd provide most of the finance. It's an attractive proposition."

"Cover yourself legally, Corinne. Although with Doug providing most of the finance, you're safe. Much of a clientele?"

"Quite considerable. It will be the only cafe, at least for a while, and there's been some demand for one in that location. I think we'd do breakfast and lunch to begin with. I'll have to quit my job."

"And if it doesn't fly?"

"Well, then I'd go back to the cafeteria, and try to work back to Assistant Manager. But Janet, we're going to make a success of this enterprise." enthused Corinne.

"That's the right attitude, Corinne. I'm sure the two of you will be successful. Just think, your own business. Yes, you've come a long way in a few months. I'm sorry I won't be here to witness your success." Then Janet put her arms around Corinne and hugged her. "I'm going to miss you, Corinne." Janet began to cry quietly.

"Oh, I'll miss you too," sobbed Corinne. "You and Claire have been such good friends. You've changed my life. You've helped me to believe in myself. If it wasn't for you two I'd still be in that "'hole in the wall' in Vancouver", to quote Claire." She began to laugh through her tears. "My favourite counselor."

"Well, at least she'll be around for a while," said Janet. "I'll send you postcards from Australia. That's a promise. I'm not much of a letter writer."

"And I'll promise to reply with postcards," grinned Corinne.

"Goodbye Corinne. Take good care of that man in your life, and don't do anything foolish."

Janet's arms slid slowly away from Corinne, and smiling through her tears, she turned and walked to the waiting bus that would take her back to the dormitory. Corinne watched until the bus was out of sight. Then she walked slowly back to her room. The sadness that filled her heart dampened her enthusiasm about her immediate future.

Ron arrived home to a boisterous, but warm welcome. Such an outpouring of feelings was new to Janet. During the brief span of meeting Ron's parents and three siblings, she was hugged more times than she had been in her twenty-four years. This spontaneous display of emotions overwhelmed her. For Janet, this was a totally new experience, and sensing her bewilderment, Ron's mother put an arm around Janet, and took her aside.

"I can see this is all a little overwhelming for you, dear." She smiled reassuringly. "We're a very demonstrative family, as you can see. The girls, especially, are delighted to see Ron back. But stick around dear. You'll get use to us."

"I'm sure I will. I like it though, all this show of emotions. When I think how I was taught to hide my emotions, I get angry."

"No stiff upper lip here," laughed Mrs. McCabe. "Now let me show you your bedroom, and I'm sure you'd like a bath or a shower."

"I'd love a hot bath. Just check on me in case I fall asleep."

"Don't worry dear. We won't let you do that."

Before having her bath, Janet met Ron's siblings, Elizabeth, the eldest, tall, like her mother, and darkly attractive. Naomi, the younger sister, was smaller than Elizabeth, and quieter, a strikingly beautiful younger version of her mother. Ron's brother, Calvin, was tall, like his father, and spoke with a pronounced Australian drawl. Along with his father, he was the driving force behind the winery. Introductions and greetings over, Jenny McCabe showed Janet upstairs to her bedroom, and then left her to the warm luxury of a bath. Next morning, after a full breakfast with Jenny McCabe and her two daughters, Janet sat down and wrote home. This initial letter home she addressed to her mother, which, she learned later, greatly incensed her father. He interpreted this as a snub, and was convinced Janet was already sharing Ron's bed. The truth was, the McCabes were very orthodox Catholics, and Ron's parents strongly disapproved of premarital sexual relations. The brothers shared a room, but each sister, and Janet had separate bedrooms.

Within a month of being at the McCabes,' Janet knew she was very much in love with Ron. One afternoon, she accompanied Elizabeth into Moorna. Having completed her business, Elizabeth suggested they have a coffee. "I have some questions to ask you, Janet."

"Oh, I think I know what's coming," Janet responded.

Elizabeth smiled. Janet anticipated her first question, which was as much a statement as a question.

"You're in love with Ron, aren't you?"

"Yes, I am. In fact, I was in love with Ron before we left Kitimat," replied Janet, rather firmly.

"How do you think you'll like being married to a grape grower, and a wine maker?"

"Elizabeth, I see myself marrying the man, Ron, not a grape grower and a wine maker. It's who he is, not what he does, that interests me."

"Touche, Janet. That was a poor question, but you're the first woman Ron's been serious about. There have been other women in his life, but you're different. You have to be for him to have invited you here. Canada's a long way from Australia."

Elizabeth looked searchingly at Janet.

"I was so happy when he asked me. I didn't want to lose him. When Ron asked me, I threw my arms around him, and that was so out of character for me. For Ron, I think that said, 'I love you.'"

"You're right, Janet. Ron wont say much about love, and being in love. He's like most Aussie males in that respect, Janet. They have difficulty with romance. They're not much for candlelight and soft music."

"Well Elizabeth, Englishmen are no different," interjected Janet.

Elizabeth smiled. "Inviting you here is Ron's way of saying 'I love you.' The actual words will come later."

"I think you're right, Elizabeth."

"Oh, he'll tell you soon enough, when he proposes, and that's coming, believe me Janet." Elizabeth smiled winsomely at Janet. "Welcome to the family."

"Well thank you, Elizabeth. I'll love being a part of your family. I need all that love and laughter. Growing up, I was starved of both."

"That's sad," said Elizabeth, "but you'll get plenty of both from the McCabes," and grinning at Janet, she added, "let's see what's happening at the McCabe household."

Elizabeth was right. Ron formally proposed to Janet two weeks after her conversation with Elizabeth. A late spring day was cooling just a little. Ron was showing Janet some recently planted Pinot Noir vines. The grapes would be used to produce a smooth wine.

"Pinot Noir is one of our best sellers," said Ron. He stopped, and looked at Janet. "Meeting you, Janet, is one of the best things that's happened to me. I'm not the most romantic person. I'm sure Elizabeth has told you."

"Yes, she did," answered Janet softly.

"What I want to say is, will you marry me?"

"Oh Ron, I've been waiting impatiently for you to ask. Of course I will," she cried, and for the second time since they met, Janet threw her arms around Ron, and hugged him.

Elizabeth was in the large lobby, when Ron and Janet returned. She looked at them, and smiled.

"So Ron, you've finally proposed."

He blushed, grinned self-consciously, and said, "Yes sis, I've finally popped the question."

"Now let's break the news to Mum and Dad, and start preparing for the big occasion." Then taking hold of Janet's hand, Elizabeth added, "Welcome to the family, Janet," and she hugged her. Elizabeth then turned to Ron, and putting her arms around him, said softly, "Congratulations Ron, you're marrying a lovely young lady."

"I think so too, sis," he said, smiling.

What pleased Janet was that her mother would be at her wedding. Janet and Ron had sent her money for the plane fare, when they learned that Janet's father had no intention of coming. "Too far! Too much money!" was his terse response when Elsie asked if he would attend his daughter's wedding. Elsie traveled to Heathrow alone, and experienced her first plane flight. Janet and Ron met her at the Adelaide train station. In spite of her fatigue, Elsie was overjoyed at seeing them. For Janet and her mother, the reunion was a tearful one, and for Elsie, the journey was one that would change her life.

"Mum, oh it's so good to see you. It's been so long," cried Janet as she hugged her mother.

"Oh it has my dear," replied her mother tearfully. "I've missed you so much."

Then Janet turned to Ron, and held his hand. "Mum, I'd like you to meet Ron, your soon-to-be son-in-law."

"Hello Mrs. Sinclair. Nice meeting you. Thanks for coming here. You've had a long journey." Ron extended his hand, and Elsie looked at him in surprise.

"Well Ron, I'm delighted to meet you, but surely you've got a hug for you soon-to-be mother-in-law?"

Smiling sheepishly, Ron hugged Elsie. "Welcome to Australia Mrs. Sinclair. Janet and I are hoping you'll stay a while."

"I'd love to, but I think my husband will have something to say about that."

"Let him," snapped Janet. "He can't come to his daughter's wedding; he's not worth going back to."

"I think we should be on our way, dear," said Elsie quietly. She noticed Ron was a little uncomfortable with this family feud.

"You're right Mum."

As they moved away to the car, Elsie put her hand on Ron's arm. He turned and looked at her, and Elsie said, "By the way Ron, call me Elsie. Mrs. Sinclair is just too formal."

"Thanks," replied Ron, a broad grin on his face. "I prefer Elsie. We Aussies are quite informal."

He quickly loaded Elsie's cases into the car, and the long drive to Moorna began. Turning to her mother in the back seat, Janet smiled, and said, "Oh mum, I'm so pleased you could come. The McCabes are excited. They think it's marvelous your coming all the way from England."

"But Janet dear, I didn't pay for the flight. I want to thank the two of you for making this possible."

"Elsie," said Ron, "it really is our pleasure. Just think, escape from an English winter."

"Oh, it's so nice to have the sunshine," replied Elsie.

"Well mum, we're hoping you'll stay. You've really nothing to go back to."

"We'll see dear. We'll see. Right now I think I'm going to sleep, if you don't mind."

"Go ahead mum. You must be tired. You've had a long journey."

Elsie's head slumped. Her eyes closed, and she fell into a deep sleep.

At ten o'clock, Ron drove down the long, curving driveway to the house. Elsie was still fast asleep. Janet called quietly, "Mum, wake-up, wake-up. We're here." Elsie stirred; opened her eyes, and looked sleepily at Janet.

"Oh, I had such a good sleep, but I could still sleep."

Ron pulled up outside the large front door. It was open, and standing in the spacious porch were Jenny and Daniel McCabe with daughter, Elizabeth. Elsie stepped out to a loud welcome. Jenny McCabe hugged her warmly, and Daniel McCabe shook her hand. "Welcome Elsie. You must be tired after your long journey."

"I am. It's wonderful to be here, but honestly, I'm ready for bed."

"Just think," said Daniel McCabe, "here all the way from England, and she wants to sleep." There was a chorus of laughter.

"Come in dear, and sit down," said Jenny. "Janet will show you to your bedroom, and if you like, I'll run your bath water."

"Oh Jenny, I'd love a bath."

"Tea before or after?" asked Jenny.

"Oh, after, thank you." Then Janet showed her mother to her bedroom, and pointed to the bathroom. Elsie could hear the water running. "Oh Janet, I'm feeling relaxed already." Minutes later she lowered herself into the warm, soothing bath water. For a few minutes, she dozed in the ample foam of the bubble bath that Jenny had put in, then for a few more minutes she relaxed in the warm comfort of the water, and thought of all that had happened over the last sixty hours of her life. She was ten thousand miles from home, and she wondered what turn her life would take in this vast country. Elsie dried herself, put on a soft bathrobe, and went downstairs into the large kitchen where Janet sat talking with Jenny and Elizabeth.

"Now that feels better, I'm sure," said Jenny.

"Baths are such luxuries," said Elsie, with a deep sigh. "Now a cup of tea, and I'll be ready for anything," and she laughed.

"How was Quantas?" asked Jenny.

"Marvelous," replied Elsie. "Their Hostesses are so attractive, and very attentive. They really help you through these long flights."

"I've heard good things about Quantas, especially their Hostesses," said Jenny.

"It's not for me," quipped Elizabeth. "I want solid ground."

"I'm inclined to agree with you, though it's such a convenient method of travel for long distances," said Janet. "Just think Mum, if you'd had to come by boat you'd still be traveling."

"Well Elizabeth, dear, I think we should leave mother and daughter alone, and see them in the morning," said Jenny.

"Yes. I'm ready for bed. Good night Elsie and Janet. See you in the morning," said Elizabeth.

"Good night to the two of you, and thank you for everything. I'm feeling at home already. In fact, this is better than home."

"Well now, Elsie," chuckled Jenny, "I think we're going to have to find a job for you."

"I wouldn't say no," replied Elsie, and Janet raised her eyebrows, and smiled.

When Jenny and Elizabeth had left, Elsie turned to Janet. "Oh my dear, it's so good to see you again. I've missed you," and she held Janet in her arms. Then she held her at arms length, and looked at her. "Being in love looks good on you," and Elsie

34

hugged Janet again. "I'm so excited about being here for your wedding. I'm truly fortunate." She smiled at Janet, and tears filled her eyes.

"Oh Mum, I'm so glad you could make it here," said Janet, embracing her mother. Then the two of them walked slowly up the stairs to their bedrooms. That night, Elsie slept contentedly.

The next morning, Elsie had breakfast with Janet and Elizabeth. Everyone else was out and busy.

"You slept well," said Elizabeth

"Oh marvelous. Must be the air. But I believe the time difference will hit me very soon."

"It probably will," offered Janet. "Ron and I took almost four days to adjust to Moorna time."

"Yes, come to think of it, the two of you didn't do much b sleep for four days after arriving," said Elizabeth, smiling. "No coffee or tea, Elsie?"

"I think I'll have coffee. New country, new habit."

"Always tea in England?" said Elizabeth.

"Yes, Elizabeth. I never tasted a good cup of coffe England."

"What would you like to eat? Boiled egg? Poached egg?

"I'll have a boiled egg, dear. But let me do that," p Elsie.

"No trouble Elsie. Toast?"

"Why yes. Thank you." Elsie was not used to such at She could not remember when she had so enjoyed such a breakfast, and with such good company. Quite suddenly good, and she was beginning to realize that returning to would be difficult, if not impossible. After breakfast, J her mother on a tour of the vineyard.

"Oh Janet, it's so big. It must require so much wo

"Yes, the pruning and the picking," replied Janet

"And so dear, you're learning all about this busir

"Yes I am. It's really interesting, and there's so much to learn."

"You know dear, I'm getting to love this place already. Maybe it's because it's so peaceful, and I'm so relaxed. No one to nag me." Elsie smiled.

"Mum, you should stay here. You've nothing to go back to. Your marriage is a disaster, if you don't mind my saying so."

"I know dear. You're right, and I don't mind your saying so. But I would need money, and so I would need a job, and who's going to employ a forty-eight-year-old woman who's never really held a job?"

"Mum, you heard Jenny say, 'We'll have to get you a job.' The McCabes know many people around here, and I'm sure they can find you a job."

"Well, I must admit, I'd love to stay. You know, Janet, you're so fortunate to be marrying into this family. They care about one another. That Jenny McCabe is a real darling."

"Oh, they're a great family. There's no doubt about that," enthused Janet. Then she took hold of her mother's arm. "Come on. I'll show you where the wine is made," and she led her to the long building that was the winery.

Finding a job for Elsie Sinclair was easier than even Janet anticipated. The lady who assisted Maggie Holmes in the Moorna Post Office was retiring after Christmas, and Maggie was looking for someone to replace her. Jenny McCabe called on Maggie, and made her request known late one afternoon, just as Maggie was closing the post office.

"Good afternoon, Maggie."

"Hello Jenny. How are you?"

"I'm fine, dear. Now I have a request of you."

"I know. You want me to sample your latest Chardonnay," laughed Maggie.

"No Maggie, I'm not calling upon your sensitive taste buds.

It's about a job for a future in-law. As you know Ron is getting married next month."

"You sent me an invitation, Jenny. I'm sure I replied. Wouldn't miss young Ron's wedding."

"Thanks Maggie, you did reply. But his mother-in-law has left a bad marriage, and she'd love to stay, but obviously needs work. She's a fine lady, Maggie, and I think she'd work well with you."

"Send her in, Jenny. I'd like to meet her. I'm sure I can arrange something for the lady."

"Oh bless you, Maggie. You're a sweetheart. I'll phone you."

"No trouble, Jenny. We have to help one another, don't we?"

"We do indeed," replied Jenny, and she looked long, and smiled at Maggie.

Two days later, Elsie sat down with Maggie Holmes. It was a Saturday morning, and Maggie closed the post office at noon.

"Elsie, let's go to The Steaming Kettle, and have a little lunch."

"That seems a good idea." Maggie had already given Elsie a preview of the post office operation, and now wanted to know what skills or training Elsie had that would prove helpful.

"I can still type. Typing is one thing I've continued to use. I type all my letters."

"That's good, Elsie. I'll get you to do any typing. I'd never make it as a typist," Maggie chuckled.

"Though my husband kept a tight reign on me, I did help at the local post office sorting Christmas mail. He liked the extra money."

"Amazing what money will do, isn't it?" Maggie said. "But your husband didn't approve of your working?"

"No Maggie. He believed my place was in the home, even when Janet was in her teens."

"Some men have a jaundiced view of women, Elsie."

"In my experience, Maggie, that's very true."

"Well Elsie, I hope you find a good new life here. I'm going to enjoy working with you."

"Thank you, Maggie. That's most encouraging."

"Now Elsie, you've got a wedding to think about. Look after that, then you can think about starting at the post office."

Elsie met Ron and Janet outside the restaurant, and together they drove back to the winery.

Janet was a beautiful bride, and both mothers sat in the front pew of the church and cried quietly. Daniel McCabe, on the other hand, beamed. To think his son was marrying such a lovely young lady, and he had to go to some remote place in Western Canada to find her. He smiled at the irony. Then Anne Marie Landor's rich soprano filled the church with the magnificent Laudate Dominum. Jenny had requested it, and her friend, who sang for the Melbourne Opera Company, obliged. Suddenly Daniel realized he too had tears in his eyes. Love each other, he thought, all the days of your lives, the way your mother and I have. Then two smiling faces turned to the people, and Ron and Janet McCabe walked down the wide aisle toward the large oak doors, to the applause of an admiring congregation

The reception was a lavish affair in the McCabe's grounds. Two marquises set end to end accommodated the eighty-four guests. Tables with parasols allowed guests to sit in the shade, and sip wine and aperitifs before enjoying the quite sumptuous lunch. The conversations were replete with compliments about the young couple, and Janet found herself blushing before the flow of well-wishers, most of whom she was meeting for the first time. During the reception, Jenny McCabe made a point of introducing Elsie to Stuart Monahan. A widower for eight years, he had been a friend of the McCabes for many more. Though tall and distinguished looking, he was a rather shy man. Jenny McCabe referred to Stuart as "the man with the winsome smile." Elsie believes that is what initially attracted her.

"England," said Stuart thoughtfully. "That's a long way to come for a wedding. Your husband's not with you?"

"No Stuart. He wouldn't come, even for his daughter's wedding."

"I can't imagine a father not attending his daughter's wedding. My wife and I never had children."

"My daughter is the single blessing of my marriage, Stuart."

"Am I detecting marital discord?"

"You are indeed."

"No hope of healing the rift?" There was a note of concern in Stuart's voice.

"None. My marriage is a mistake I've lived with for twenty-five years."

"That's too long to live with that kind of mistake. I wonder you didn't divorce years ago."

"My husband wouldn't consider one, so we have just lived our separate lives, and I have grown very close to Janet."

"Will you stay here," Stuart asked.

"I will, now that Jenny McCabe has arranged a job for me at the local post office."

"Oh, you're going to be working with Maggie Holmes," said Stuart, smiling.

"Obviously you know her?"

"Oh, everyone knows Maggie. She's a great lady. You'll enjoy working with her."

"I'm getting that impression."

"When do you start?"

"After the wedding. I'll go in on Monday."

"That's wonderful. So I can expect to see more of you?"

"Well, I suppose so." Elsie was a little surprised by the remark.

Suddenly Janet was at her mother's side. "Now this looks like a serious conversation." She linked arms with her mother, and chuckled.

"Actually dear it is. Mr. Monahan is encouraging me to stay, and I have told him I now intend to."

"It's a great idea, Mr. Monahan, don't you think?"

"Indeed I do. By the way, it's Stuart. Mister is so formal."

"But," replied Janet, "I can just hear my father's reaction, but I suppose a wife can legally leave her husband. You know, incompatibility I believe it's called."

"My goodness, Janet, just married, and you're plotting your mother's separation from her husband." Stuart laughed softly.

"If only you knew, Stuart," said Janet, seriously. "It should have happened a long time ago."

"Well ladies, it's getting late, and I must leave. I've so enjoyed talking with you. I'm sure we will meet again. Congratulations on your marriage, Janet, and Elsie, success in your new job."

"Nice meeting you Stuart," echoed Elsie and Janet in unison, and they watched Stuart stride away to his vehicle.

Recognizing Elsie's situation, the McCabes dispensed with protocol, and put on a lavish meal for their guests, who raved about the sea- food dishes. "The dinner," they said, "was typical of the McCabes' generosity," and Elsie expressed her appreciation tearfully.

"Elsie," said Jenny, after the last of the guests had said their farewells, "you are more than welcome. Dan and I are so delighted that Ron has married such a lovely young lady, and yours is a difficult situation. We are pleased to help out."

"It's so kind of you," said Elsie, tearfully, as Jenny put a comforting arm around her shoulder.

Just then, Janet appeared. She held Jenny's hands. "Thank you so much for a beautiful reception," and she began to cry in Jenny's arms.

"You're very welcome, my dear. It's really been a pleasure doing it."

"I heard nothing but compliments about the food, and, of course, the wine. Do you realize the reputation you have around here?"

"Well, you know Janet, dear. If you're good to people, they'll return that in different ways," replied Jenny.

"Oh my," said a grateful Elsie, "I've certainly come to the right place."

At the post office, Elsie rose to the occasion. She worked hard to learn all that was involved in operating a rural post office. She enjoyed the work, as well as Maggie, her jovial co-worker. The two of them became an effective tandem, and the locals were greatly amused by their witty banter. For the first time in her life Elsie was experiencing genuine independence, and she was not about to relinquish it to a failed marriage. Stuart offered Elsie a room in his spacious three-bedroom house a mile outside Moorna, but she declined. For her, such an arrangement was unacceptable. She liked Stuart, but felt that when she slept in his house, it would be as his wife. The alternative, which she accepted, was to have a room in Maggie's house, and to share the cooking. This was a convenient arrangement, and the two became close friends, delighting in demonstrating their culinary talents.

"I haven't tasted such delicious Beef Wellington," said Elsie one evening

"Well dearie," replied a smiling Maggie, "Your quiche was truly the best I've eaten. There's a real art to making a good quiche. I've eaten too many soft, runny ones."

"A toast," proposed Elsie, "to appetizing cuisine."

"Now I'll drink to that," laughed Maggie.

A month after Elsie began working at the post office she received a letter from her husband. She had sent him a post office box address. The news was not good. After suffering through a series of debilitating headaches, William went to his doctor, who sent him to a specialist. The diagnosis was a brain tumor, and the prognosis was not good. William asked Elsie to return as soon as possible. When Elsie informed Janet of her father's condition, her response was blunt. "I don't believe him. Tell him you want signed, witnessed letters from both his doctor and the specialist. He'll do anything to get you back."

"Oh, he'll have some good reason why he can't do that, I'll go back. Maybe he'll agree to the divorce I've wanted for so long."

"No letters, no return," snapped Janet.

"I'll go. He's so stubborn," replied her mother.

"Mum, if it's a lie, Ron and I will send you the airfare. Better still, we'll give you the money before you leave."

"You don't have to do that, dear. I'll get back, even if I have to go by boat."

"No mum, Ron and I won't hear of that."

"It's a lot of money, Janet."

"We can afford it, mum."

"Thank you dear. That's very kind of you."

"Oh mum, you're worth it. You've been a wonderful mother."

Janet hugged her mother, who remained in Janet's arms a long moment, before letting go, and wiping tears from her eyes. A little later, Maggie assured Elsie she would still have her job when she returned.

"From what you've told me, Elsie, I think you're going to be back. Just don't be too long. I miss your cooking." They laughed together.

Two days later, Elsie was on a plane for England. Predictably, William was not at the airport to meet her. When did he ever put himself out for me? she thought. The train to Estley made only two stops, so the final stage of her long journey passed quickly. It was dark when she arrived, so she took a taxi to the house. Then, filled with trepidation, she stood before the front door. She paused before knocking nervously. There was a movement from within, and suddenly the door opened.

"Hello Willie," said Elsie softly. "How are you?"

"I'm fine. Why do you ask?" His voice was almost a sneer.

"Well why do you think I'm here?"

"Oh, you mean my letter," he replied indifferently.

"Well of course," replied Elsie, clearly irritated. "You said you had a brain tumor, and you wanted me back."

His response was a silly grin.

"You look pretty good for a man with a brain tumor."

"I don't have a brain tumor," he replied curtly.

"Then you lied. How cruel and thoughtless of you. Janet said you were lying." Elsie was visibly annoyed.

"Well, I had to get you back somehow, otherwise you'd probably have stayed in Australia," he replied angrily.

"And you chose to lie to get me back. How despicable. There's no love between us. You've no respect for me." Elsie began to cry.

"Well, we'll just have to get along without love," said William indifferently.

"I'm not living with a man who no longer loves me."

"And where do you think you'll go?" replied William smugly. "Remember I have the money."

"I'll go back to Australia. I have the money."

"Oh my, a little sex for money on the side," sneered William.

"You're disgusting. I have a daughter and a son-in-law who care about me. I don't need you, Willie" There was a note of triumph in her voice.

"Well go then. You'll not get a damn thing from me," snarled Willie.

"The only thing I want from you is a divorce." Elsie's voice was now soft and firm.

"I wont give you that," replied Willie vindictively.

"You're spiteful enough to do that, aren't you?"

Willie's response was a foolish grin.

Not wanting to stay in the house with a man she despised, Elsie turned, and started walking away.

"Don't come running back," he shouted.

Elsie paused, and turned. "Whatever makes you think I would do that?"

"Oh, I know you."

"No you don't, Willie. You've never really known me. All I've ever been is a convenience in your bed." With that, she turned, and walked quickly away. Willie watched speechlessly as Elsie disappeared down the street. This was the last he would ever see of her.

Elsie was fortunate. She was able to purchase a seat someone had cancelled, and two days after arriving in England, she was on her way back to Australia. She was, she told herself, going home.

When the plane touched down at the Sydney Airport, Elsie experienced a great sense of relief, not because of a safe landing, but because she felt she was home. Soon she would be reunited with Janet and good friends. She vowed never to return to England. Australia was now her home. She had had a long time to think about her life, especially more recent events- meeting the McCabes and Stuart, and her job with Maggie. She would marry Stuart tomorrow if her spiteful husband would agree to a divorce, and she didn't want to wait seven years for her marriage to be declared null and void. Maybe she could force Willie to agree to a divorce. She knew he would be looking for every opportunity to have an affair. At this thought she felt her anger growing. She looked out at the spectacular scenery of the Great Divide, so different from the monotony of her home in England. As she sat absorbing the beauty, she began to sense the vastness of this land. Beyond this rugged beauty, she thought, lies the desert. Endless sand beneath a shimmering heat, and dry, salt lakes. This was not the quiet, gentle beauty of England, with its quaint villages. This Australia was a vast, trackless land, with most of its people strung out along its eastern shoreline. She had also learned that those who lived in the arid areas were a hardy breed. Her eyes grew heavy; her head slumped to the side, and she fell fast asleep. Two hours later, she awakened suddenly to the sounds of activity in the car. Passengers were pulling down their cases, and moving toward the exit doors. Elsie rose shakily to her feet, and looked up at her suitcases. A tall, young man smiled at her and said, "I'll take those down for you mam," and he swung them to the floor with ease.

"Why, thank you."

"No trouble. First visit to Adelaide?"

"No, I've been once before, but not to visit. I'm going on to Moorna."

"Nice little town. There's a great winery there. The McCabe family owns it. Nice people".

"I believe so," replied Elsie, a twinkle in her eyes.

Just then the train jerked to a stop, and passengers began crowding toward the doors.

"Well enjoy Moorna, and visit the winery." The obliging young man smiled at Elsie as he swung his pack on to his shoulder.

"Oh, I will," said Elsie returning his smile.

"Here, let me carry those for you," and once again, Elsie was the beneficiary of the young man's thoughtfulness. With the same consummate ease with which he took them down, he carried Elsie's suitcases off the train, and placed them on the platform. She followed, mutely grateful, as, with a wave, he disappeared.

"Mum." She would know that voice anywhere, and looking up she saw Janet running toward her, followed by Ron. Next moment she was in Janet's tearful embrace.

"Oh, it's so good to have you back. You didn't waste any time."

"No I didn't, and it's so good to be back. Hello Ron dear. Good to see you again."

"Well Elsie, it's good to have you back here again. Lets hope you're staying."

"Oh, I'm staying all right," and she hugged him.

"Now, there's someone else to see you," said Janet, smiling broadly.

Elsie followed Janet's gaze, and standing nearby, tall and smiling, was Stuart.

"How nice of you to come, Stuart. Nice to see you again."

"Good to have you back," and he gave Elsie a hug, which she

received gratefully. "Now, I hope you're up for a long drive. It's a long way to Moorna."

"I know. I've done it once before," replied Elsie.

"That's right. I was forgetting."

"You can sleep mum, if you feel like it."

"I probably will, though right now I'm too excited to sleep. I've lots to tell you."

"Don't tell me. Dad's agreed to a divorce?"

"No such luck. He's as adamant as ever. 'You'll not get a divorce out of me.' But he's not going without female company. I'm certain of that."

"Maybe one of his female companions will persuade him to do so." Stuart added his insight.

"Don't I hope." There was a look of longing in Elsie's eyes.

"But mum, he was lying about the tumor, wasn't he?"

"Yes dear, you were right. He was lying. Our encounter was short and bitter. He'll never see me again."

"Thank God for that," said Janet, clearly relieved. "You just have to get that damn divorce."

"Now on a more pleasant note," interrupted Stuart, "Maggie's looking forward to seeing you again, having you back at the post office, and most of all tasting your cooking."

Elsie laughed. "She's such a sweetheart. I've missed her." Then she went quiet, and very soon she was asleep.

Maggie was getting ready to close the post office when Elsie arrived. She turned around as Elsie entered, and a smile lit up her face. Arms outstretched, Maggie moved quickly to embrace Elsie.

"Welcome back Elsie dear. I knew you would be back. I've missed you, not to mention your cooking," she laughed.

"I've missed you too, Maggie. I've missed the laughs."

"I guess you didn't have any in England."

"You can say that again. Nothing but harsh words."

"And I bet you didn't get a divorce."

"No. Not a hope."

"Well Elsie, your job's still here. When do you think you'll start?"

"How about tomorrow?"

"Oh, take a day or two to get over your travel. Now lets go and have some tea, and you can tell me all your news."

"Tea sounds good," said Elsie. Maggie locked up, and they were soon seated in the comfortable confines of The Steaming Kettle.

Elsie related her unpleasant encounter with William, and his firm, curt refusal for a divorce.

"Maybe he'll meet someone, and change his mind," suggested Maggie.

"My God! Who would want him, Maggie?"

"You never know, Elsie. He obviously has a need of female company, and he may just ingratiate himself to some woman. I'll bet he was seeing someone while you were away."

"You think so Maggie? You think a woman would fall for him?"

"Elsie, you did," replied Maggie with a soft smile.

"You're right, though the feeling didn't last long. But if he gets all the sex he wants, he'll be happy."

"That's right. Doesn't take much to keep some men happy." Maggie laughed heartily.

"Well Maggie, lets hope he finds someone who keeps him happy. Then he might give me a divorce."

"Here's hoping, Elsie," said Maggie, grinning.

Elsie sipped her tea, a wistful look on her face. "Yes, here's hoping. Now Maggie, I'm going to finish unpacking, and get a good night's sleep. Then I'll see you in the morning."

"No rush, dearie, but I'll certainly appreciate your company."

They walked outside, and took a taxi home.

Stuart Monahan was a frequent visitor to Moorna now that Elsie was back. On a number of occasions he invited Elsie to his home for dinner, and gave Elsie a sample of his considerable culinary skills. She grew very fond of him. There was a genuine gentleness about his manner that she loved. If only Willie would agree to a damn divorce, she thought. If only he would meet that woman who would give him what he wanted. Meanwhile, she enjoyed Stuart's company. They did everything except sleep together.

Maggie was a perfect work mate for Elsie. Maggie made her laugh, and took her mind off Willie, and his spiteful stubbornness.

"You've got a good man in Stuart," Maggie reminded Elsie one day, "and Willie will never know if you share Stuart's bed. Come to think of it, he probably wouldn't give a damn."

"Oh, you're probably right, Maggie. I just don't want to give him any benefit if ever we do divorce. If I'm asked, 'Have you ever slept with Mr. Monahan?' I want to be able to say 'No.'"

"You've got a point, Elsie, and you've got more will power than I have," Maggie chuckled. "But lets go and have some lunch."

"I'm ready for that," replied Elsie.

Janet was settling into married life with unexpected ease, probably because Ron made no unnecessary demands on her. The two of them seemed to have an awareness of each other's needs, and how to meet them. They had moved into a two-bedroom house close to the vineyard, and Janet had taken upon herself the job of accountant-bookkeeper, for which Ron's father and her brother-in-law, Calvin, were deeply grateful.

"Janet," said Calvin one day, "thanks for looking after the books. It's one part of this whole operation we've been lax about. You're doing a great job organizing the finances, and I want you to know we're very grateful."

"Well thanks, Calvin. I just wanted to make myself useful."

"You're good value sis," said Calvin, a smile spreading slowly over his face.

Janet was determined to acquaint herself with all aspects of the vineyard and the winery. From the brothers she learned about the different kinds of grapes, and which ones were used to produce the winery's renowned chardonnay. All this was a formidable task, but slowly she was learning.

"You know darling," said Ron, "soon you'll know more about this wine business than any of us."

"Then, my dear, we'll have to consider renaming the winery." She laughed at his surprised look.

For the first time in her life Janet felt part of a family whose members cared for, and loved one another. Clare was thousands of miles away, but now Janet had Elizabeth, who was like a sister

She enjoyed the family gatherings, and especially Sundays when the McCabe family would gather around the dinner table laden with food, offer a sincere grace, and then relish the food and wine. Elsie and Stuart were often guests on these occasions, and before an embarrassed Stuart, she would condone bigamy by her mother. It pained Janet to see a couple like her mother and Stuart so in love, but unable to marry because a spiteful, stubborn husband in England would not agree to a divorce.

"Oh mum, be a bigamist. Dad will never know, and we're the only ones who'll ever know you are."

"But others will dear, and if banns are read in church, your in-laws would have difficulty compromising their consciences."

"I suppose you're right," replied Janet glumly.

"Well Janet, from what you've told me about your father, I don't think Elsie will have long to wait before he's asking for a divorce," said Elizabeth.

"You know, Elizabeth," said Elsie, "you're the second person in two weeks to say that. I'm beginning to think it just might happen," and she placed a hand on Stuart's arm, and smiled.

"I think we should drink to that," suggested Calvin dryly.

Suddenly eight glasses were raised in unison. "To mum's divorce," said Janet enthusiastically.

There was a clink of glasses, and everyone drank the toast.

"Well, I must say, as a practicing Catholic, I never thought I would drink to someone's hoped for divorce," chuckled Jenny McCabe.

"Father Corrigan would be a little concerned," added her husband, smiling. "But for Elsie's sake, I hope the divorce happens."

Three days later, with Maggie at the dentist for an early appointment, Elsie opened the post office. One of the first things she did was to check if she had any mail. She did, surprisingly, a letter from Willie. What on earth could be so important for him to write? she thought. She opened the letter, began reading, and became so excited she rushed to the phone to call Janet, who was about to leave the house to go to the winery.

"Hello mum. It's early to call, isn't it?"

"Oh darling, the best news in years," said Elsie, excitedly.

"Oh, don't tell me! Dad's finally agreed to a divorce?"

"Yes. He says he's met a highly compatible lady, and he's ready to give me a divorce. Oh, I'm so excited."

"So mum, this means he's met a woman who'll give him all the sex he wants."

"You're probably right, Janet. Who cares? I get the divorce I've wanted. I'll be free to marry Stuart, and your father can have all the sex he desires"

"So he's settled for sex, and not love," said Janet caustically.

"Of course dear. He doesn't know what love is. I hope they'll be happy, though I don't think the woman knows what she's getting into."

"Mum, I want to be sure you get a fair market price for your share of the house. I'm going to contact Mr. Goodwin. I'm sure he will help us."

"Thank you Janet. I'd appreciate that. Now I have to phone Stuart, and arrange a wedding.."

"Mum, hold on. You're not divorced yet, and you have to find a minister who will perform the ceremony."

"Oh, I'm just so excited. This is so unexpected. I can't wait to tell Stuart." Elsie was almost breathless with excitement. "But you know dear, he'll be thrilled when he hears my good news."

"Oh mum, I'm so pleased you've at last met a man who truly loves you. Now I have to go. Maybe I'll drop around tonight, and we'll have a glass of wine to celebrate. Love you mum."

"I love you too, dear." Elsie heard the phone click at the other end, then, she too, hung up.

Elsie was right. Stuart was excited to hear her good news, and arranged to meet her at the Steaming Kettle later that morning.

When Maggie arrived at the post office, Elsie greeted her excitedly. She took hold of Maggie's hands.

"Oh Maggie, you'll never guess what's happened. Something absolutely wonderful." Elsie's face was radiant.

"Well my dear, for you to be so excited, and looking so radiant, I have to say your Willie's agreed to a divorce."

"Yes! Yes! You're absolutely correct. Oh Maggie, isn't it just the best news?"

"To that I have to say, yes. Elsie, I'm so happy for you, and also for Stuart."

"Do you mind? I'm meeting him later this morning at the Steaming Kettle."

"Wonderful idea. I might even close shop for a while and help you celebrate. That means a wedding coming up," and Maggie gave Elsie a hug. "So Elsie, your Willie's met some hussy who's going to give him what he wants, and he's decided to let go, and two lovely people who love each other can now get married. I think that's great. And it's time you went over to the Kettle."

"Thank you, Maggie. See you in a little while."

At eleven o'clock, Stuart stepped into the Steaming Kettle, and hugged a smiling, excited Elsie.

"Well Elsie, now I can propose to you," and he smiled as he bowed histrionically.

"You may, my dear," giggled Elsie.

"Should I go down on bended knee?"

"Oh darling, you can stand on your head if you wish."

Then Stuart looked at Elsie, a soft smile on his lips. "Marry me, Elsie."

"Oh, Stuart, those are the sweetest words I've heard in a long time. Of course I will," and she fell into his arms, and looking up, kissed him on the lips.

"Oh my, oh my, it's happened at last. I do believe Stuart has proposed, and we've got a wedding coming up." Judy, the young proprietress of the Steaming Kettle had just emerged from her office. "This calls for a celebration, even at eleven in the morning. I happen to have a bottle of McCabe's Chardonnay," and she went to the wine rack, and returned with the Chardonnay, and four wine glasses.

"Four glasses?" said Stuart.

"Yes," replied Judy. "I'll bet Maggie walks in at any moment."

She was right. Barely was the cork out of the bottle, and Maggie entered, a broad smile on her face.

"You didn't think I was going to miss this toast, did you?"

As Father Corrigan would not approve officiating at the marriage of a divorced woman, Elsie and Stuart approached the pastor of a local Pentacostal church. Elsie explained her situation, and found the young pastor sympathetic. They would attend six sessions on Christian marriage, and the pastor asked them to attend the Sunday service, and consider joining the church. The following Sunday, Elsie and Stuart attended their first service at Moorna Pentacostal Church. For both of them the experience was a revelation. Use to the solemn liturgy of both the Church of England and the Catholic Church, Elsie and Stuart found the exuberant praise and worship spiritually energizing. "I like it," whispered Elsie near the end of the service. Then as they left the sanctuary, she added, "There's a freedom here I never experienced in the church at home. I think in time, I'll raise my hands."

"I'll probably take a little longer," said Stuart. "But I see people really use their Bibles. In the Catholic Church I grew up in, the priest never said, 'open your Bibles.' They were like an appendage."

As they walked into the spacious foyer, Pastor Stanley Kennedy was there to greet them, and shake their hands warmly. "I'm so glad you came, and I trust you'll return," he said enthusiastically.

"We certainly will," replied Stuart. "It's good to be here. Already we've been invited to join a study group, and I have an invitation to the next Men's Breakfast."

"That's always a good function," added Pastor Kennedy. "I look forward to seeing you there, and I'll be meeting with the two of you on Thursday evening for the first of the sessions on Christian Marriage. So, until then Elsie and Stuart, God bless you."

As Elsie and Stuart turned to leave, a heavy man with a florid complexion greeted them with an infectious laugh. "I'm Edward Gilbert. You're obviously new to the church. Welcome." He extended a large hand, which Stuart quickly shook.

"I'm Stuart Monahan, and this is my fiancée, Elsie Sinclair."

"Pleased to meet you Elsie. I believe you're from England?"

"Yes, I am."

"I believe congratulations are in order," and sensing Elsie's surprise, he added, "I'm an elder of the church, so I get to know about these things before others. Be assured, I wont say anything before the banns are announced."

"Thank you, "said Elsie. "We'd appreciate that."

Just then, a tall, rather heavyset lady with smiling blue eyes came alongside Edward. He looked at her admiringly. "And this lady is my wife, Margaret. Dear, this lady is Elsie, and this handsome gentleman is her fiancé, Stuart. They've just joined the church, and in September they are to be married. But, my dear, not a word until the banns are published."

"Oh, you can rely on me. Congratulations to both of you. But Elsie, permit me to be nosey, a woman's prerogative," and she smiled at Elsie. "Is this the first marriage for both of you?"

Edward was clearly embarrassed. "Now dear, you're being rather personal."

"Oh, don't worry Edward," replied Elsie, "people will find out soon enough. To answer your question, Margaret, it's the second for both of us. Stuart is a widower, and I'm a divorcee."

"Well, I hope you will be very happy together. Looking at you, I'm sure you will," replied Margaret affectionately.

"Thank you. I can assure you we will," said Stuart, as he placed a reassuring arm around Elsie's waist.

"Well, it's good to have you in our church, and it's been good talking with you," said Edward.

"It has indeed," added Margaret. "Elsie, we'll have to meet one afternoon for tea at The Steaming Kettle. I'm sure you know it." By now she was holding both Elsie's hands in hers. Then just as quickly, she let go, took hold of her husband's arm, and together they strode almost regally out of the church. Elsie and Stuart looked at each other with broad grins on their faces, and followed them out.

"I think we've made a good choice, Elsie," Stuart remarked, as they went slowly down the broad front steps.

"I think you're right, dear," replied Elsie with a smile.

Janet wrote to Edward Goodwin explaining her mother's situation. She had three pertinent questions: Is it possible for two people living thousands of miles apart to divorce? May one party of the divorce withdraw her equity in a house, even though the other party continues to live in the dwelling? Will your firm be willing to provide legal service for my mother?

Janet assured Mr. Goodwin that she, and her husband would pay all legal costs. Edward Goodwin was quick to reply. Initially, he sent a telegram to the Moorna Post Office. It read: Delighted to assist with legal services. Yes to all questions. Letter to follow. Edward Goodwin.

In the letter that followed, Edward Goodwin informed Janet that he had assigned a very bright young lawyer, new to the firm, to her mother's case. His name was Lester Thomas. The divorce would be a slow process because of the numerous forms to be signed and witnessed. What helped accelerate this ponderous process was William Sinclair's admission of adultery. He too, was eager to accomplish his second marriage. "Excluding unforeseen problems," wrote Mr. Goodwin, "the divorce should be finalized early in August. The financial settlement may take a little longer. But plan for a wedding in late August, or early September. " This was encouraging to Elsie, though she worried about the legal costs.

"Mum, don't worry. Ron and I will take care of the costs."

"But I should be paying for my divorce, not you and Ron. I'm sure Stuart will help."

"Mum, start thinking about a wedding. Forget about the cost of your divorce."

When Elsie mentioned the matter of legal costs for her divorce to Stuart, he was quick to assure her that he would take care of that.

"That's very kind of you dear. But I must contribute something," replied a rather anxious Elsie.

In England, William Sinclair smiled as he contemplated Elsie's legal expenses for employing so prestigious a London law firm as Compton, Goodwin, and James. Following his first meeting with Lester Thomas, he had made enquiries about the firm. Their legal costs left him wondering why he had not pursued a career in the legal profession. The expenses involved in a divorce such as his and Elsie's were formidable. He had chosen a local lawyer, whose fee, he knew, would be significantly less than Elsie's. But she wanted it, so she would pay for it. What William Sinclair was never to know was that Elsie's legal process was done "pro bono" as Edward Goodwin's wedding gift to the future Mrs. Elsie Monahan.

The sessions with Pastor Kennedy proved stimulating. He spoke about a contract not only between two people, but also one involving God, "and that," he said, "is the big difference between a church wedding and a civil one. Always keep God in your relationship," he emphasized. They read much, and discussed extensively, and Stuart and Elsie developed a deep appreciation for the young pastor. It seemed that all they discussed over the six weeks was a part of Pastor Kennedy's marriage, and accounted for the careful balance he maintained between his married life, and his role as pastor of a growing, dynamic young church.

The marriage banns were announced late in July, and the wedding took place on a warm, sunny Saturday, early in September. A few cirrus clouds drifting across a blue sky, and a soft breeze were early harbingers of spring. By 9.30 the church was almost full. Many of the women from the church were present, and also many of Stuart's friends, as well as Elsie's growing number of friends and acquaintances, Maggie, of course, prominent in the front row. With Ron as best man, it seemed only appropriate that Elizabeth was Elsie's maid of honour. When the moment came for the exchange of vows, Maggie placed her hand on Janet's, and the two looked at each other tearfully, and when the vows were concluded, she squeezed Janet's hand affectionately.

The reception was held in the gaily- decorated church hall, the food provided by a highly recommended local caterer. Before Elsie and Stuart sat down, Janet came up and placed an arm around each of them. "You've waited a long time for this day, mum. Relish it, and enjoy all your days with Stuart. May they be many." Then, having hugged the two of them, she wiped the tears from her eyes. Before leaving them to the congratulations of the noisy guests, Janet put her arms around her mother, and held her close, almost reluctant to let go. "Oh Mum, I'm so happy for you. This is such a wonderful day. You've found someone who truly loves you." Then she looked at Stuart, standing tall and smiling beside

Elsie. "Thank you Stuart for bringing love into my mother's life. I know you'll have a beautiful life together."

Stuart smiled at her. "Looks like I've adopted a wonderful daughter." Then he hugged her. Shortly after, Stuart and Elsie were acknowledging the enthusiastic congratulations of the excited guests. At one point, Elsie turned to Stuart and said, "You know darling, you'd think I had lived here all my life." Stuart's smile was mute acknowledgment.

The following day, Stuart and Elsie loaded two suitcases into their station wagon, and began their honeymoon- a tour of Victoria State. In Melbourne, Elsie thought she was back in England. The trams, and many of the buildings had a distinctly English appearance, but not the people. "They are unmistakably Australian," said Elsie.

"Is that good?" asked Stuart, smiling.

"Absolutely," laughed Elsie.

Along that straight stretch of golden sand, The Ninety-Mile Beach, they made frequent stops, and Elsie walked bare-foot on the sand, and let the sea wash over her feet. She closed her eyes, and pirouetted along the golden sand. She experienced a wonderful sense of freedom from all that had inhibited her in the past. Stuart watched, and an intense feeling of love consumed him. Eight years a widower, he never thought he would meet someone who would fill the void created by Justine's death. Then Elsie came into his life, and his world changed, as did Elsie's. He watched her frolic with the uninhibited joy of a child, and smiled.

"It's moments like this that make me wish we lived close to the sea. There's something soothing and restful about the sea."

"You're right about that, Elsie," replied Stuart reflectively. "It has its own magic. It's such a vast, restless force that never sleeps."

"Darling, that's very poetic," said Elsie, and she nestled up to Stuart. "Oh darling, I can't recall ever feeling so happy."

"Well Elsie, I haven't felt such happiness in over eight years. I didn't think I would experience such happiness again after

Justine died. Thank you, my dear, for bringing this joy back into my life."

"We've been so fortunate to have found each other," said Elsie, "and all thanks to my daughter with a wander lust."

They linked arms, and wandered along the beach before turning back to the car. A light breeze was coming off the ocean, and woolly cumulus clouds were gathering in the southern sky.

"I'm ready for some dinner," said Stuart.

"Dinner sounds like a good idea. I'm hungry," said Elsie. "It's all this sea air."

They drove a short distance to a hotel that served a succulent rack-of-lamb, which they washed down with a dry red wine. After dinner, they sat on the verandah, sipped sherry, and listened to the sounds of evening, and smelled the fragrance of magnolia.

"Thank you Stuart for a wonderful day. I'm not use to such courtesy."

"Well, my dear, you're so deserving of it. It really was my pleasure."

"I so enjoyed being on the beach. I can't remember when I last walked on sand. I must have been fifteen when I first stood on a beach, and saw the ocean. My parents didn't travel much. No car. We relied on buses and trains, and living in Buckinghamshire, the sea was remote. My father thought the countryside had enough beauty, and mother never objected. Today was magic. I just had to dance and laugh."

"It's good to let your feelings take over," said Stuart. "Sometimes we need to become children again, and let our feelings run free."

"You know, Stuart, I can't remember when I last did something like that. Oh, it was wonderful." Elsie closed her eyes, and smiled.

"You'll have to do it again," chuckled Stuart. "You look so beautiful when you dance."

"And now, darling," said Elsie, "I'm ready for bed."

How different this night was from those with Willie, when

he would maul her body, breathlessly satisfy his sexual need, then roll off Elsie, and fall asleep. For her the whole act was distasteful and inconsiderate. Elsie always felt used and demeaned. Tonight, no seeking her breasts and thighs. Instead, a gentle embrace, and goodnight kiss, and then quite spontaneously, sleep. Their love- making would come another time, gentle, loving, mutually passionate and satisfying.

Elsie and Stuart awakened to the early morning sun pouring into their room. After a light breakfast, they drove north through the Australian Alps to Wangaratta. At six thousand feet the air was thinner and cooler. Elsie had never experienced such altitude, or such rugged beauty. They returned to Moorna along the northern border of Victoria, stopping at towns nestled on the banks of the Murray River. After more than fourteen days on the road, Elsie appreciated her new home and bed. She phoned Maggie, and invited her over for lunch. Though it was Saturday, Stuart had gone into the office to look at plans for a new highway project he was involved in. Maggie closed the post office at noon, and by 12:30 she was seated in Elsie's bright sun- room, an appetizing lunch set before her.

"Hello Elsie dear. You needn't have gone to all this trouble. This is quite luxurious. Something tells me you have been eating in high style. You look like a well loved, well satisfied woman," laughed Maggie.

"You're right on both counts," replied a beaming Elsie. "Oh Maggie, the whole trip was beautiful. Stuart treated me like a queen."

"In his eyes, dearie, you are. He recognizes how fortunate he is."

Then Elsie looked at Maggie, her eyes shining, a smile lighting up her face. "But you know, Maggie, I never knew sex could be so wonderful."

Maggie burst out laughing. "Now I'm jealous, Elsie. I must say; you do surprise me. There's fire in you yet, my dear," and she continued to laugh.

Elsie continued to look at Maggie, but now with a tenderness in her eyes. "Maggie, my dear, were you never in love?"

Maggie's Story.

In the summer of 1939 I was madly in love with a young, handsome bush pilot, Geoff. Newcombe. Oh, he was a lovely man, Elsie, gentle, and soft-spoken. Flying was one of his passions. I was the other. Then came Dunkirk, and Geoff said he had to go. England needed young, experienced pilots, and he wanted to fly fighter planes. He traveled to America, met up with some Americans who were doing the same thing, and together they flew to England. He joined the R.A.F., and flew out of Biggin Hill. He wrote as often as he could. I still have all his letters. So many sad stories; so many of those young men died, shot down in their youth, or surviving with terrible burns. But many of the letters were beautiful. He never failed to say how much he loved me, and how he missed me, and that he was being faithful to me. I believed him. He was that kind of man.

"How wonderful, Maggie," interrupted Elsie. "Not many men would have remained faithful, especially in those circumstances."

Then, in September 1943, he was shot down over northern France. He managed to bail out, but was quickly captured, and sent to the infamous Stalag Luft III prison camp. Many Air Force pilots were sent there. In February 1944 he was part of "The Great Escape" from Stalag Luft III, and was one of the fifty recaptured prisoners murdered on Hitler's orders.

"I remember that, Maggie. People in England were horrified. I believe some of those guilty of murdering prisoners were hunted down after the war, and were executed."

"You're right, Elsie. The man who murdered Geoff was one of them, but it didn't bring Geoff back."

Maggie's Story continued.

When I finally received the news from the War Office, I cried myself to sleep for days

"There was no one else after Geoff, Maggie?"

Oh, a couple of casual dates, but I was looking for Geoff, and he wasn't there. I used to re-read his last letter to me. It was so beautiful, so full of love and hope. He told me how much he loved me, how much he missed me, but he also wrote about all we would do when he returned. He had such wonderful dreams. Then one bullet from a murderer's gun, and the dreams ended.

Some years before, in 1940, I became a driver for high-ranking military personnel. One was a general. He commanded the army group that fought in New Guinea. He knew about Geoff, and how he had flown in the Battle of Britain, and was immensely proud of what Geoff had done.

'They are real heroes,' he told me one day. 'Men like Geoff answered the call,' he said. 'They didn't wait to be called.' The general was very good to me, and when I told him about Geoff's murder, following the escape, he had tears in his eyes. 'Murdering bastards,' he said, angrily. 'We have to get on with the job of winning this war.' Then he told me to take a few days off." 'You need time to grieve, Maggie. I'm so sorry. Your Geoff was a real hero. I would have liked to have met him.' In May of '45 I took over the post office here in Moorna. I answered an ad, and the general gave me a glowing recommendation. I became quite absorbed in the work of reorganizing the whole operation, and making it what one magazine writer described as 'the best rural post office in the state of Victoria.' So here I am, Elsie, happy spinster, and likely to remain so.

"Such a sad love story," said Elsie.

"For one brief summer, I experienced a wonderful love, Elsie. Maybe that's all I'm meant to experience. Just think. It will never change. That love will always be what it was for the summer of 1939." Maggie smiled.

"Maggie, you'll always be my very dear friend." Tears filled Elsie's eyes.

"And yours is a friendship I'll always treasure, Elsie. Now before we get too sentimental, pour me a glass of that Chardonay."

Five weeks after her wedding, Elsie received a most unexpected letter from William.

"What on earth could he want?" asked a bemused Elsie. "For him to write he must want something."

"He wants you back," said Stuart.

"No, not now he has a most compatible lady."

"Maybe she's not so compatible after all," smiled Stuart.

Elsie opened the letter, and began to read silently. Stuart watched her smile spread. "You know darling, you're right. The compatible lady has obviously discovered the real William Sinclair, and she's left him. But listen to this, dear:

'I realize I was not a good husband to you, but I know I can change. With your help, Elsie, I know I can. So I'm asking you to please come back into my life. Divorces can be nullified. Together, I believe we can have a good life.'

"Does he really think I will ever consider returning to him? 'Don't come running back,' said he. Well William Sinclair, I wont." There was contempt in Elsie's voice. "He just doesn't understand."

"Will you bother to reply, dear?"

"Oh yes, darling, brief and to the point. I'm going to enjoy this."

Elsie's reply was terse indeed. There was no salutation.

I will never return to you, William, nor will I ever return to England. I am enjoying the real love of a wonderful man, and for the first time in my life, I am truly happy.

Goodbye,

Mrs. Elsie Monahan.

On a sunny morning, early in October, the trees tinged with autumn colours, sunshine streaming through the window of the front room, William George Sinclair sat down and read the letter from his ex-wife. It was brief, and for a moment, he sat as though stunned. Then, for the first time in his memory, William George Sinclair cried.